THIS BOOK BELONGS TO

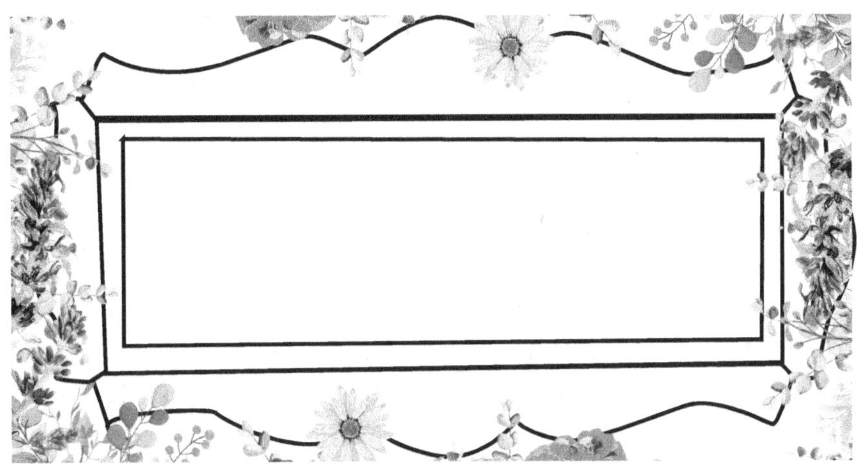

CHAPTER 1:

When the girl said that she had been held captive for a month and forcibly physically abused by a monster-shaped vampire,

no one paid attention to her, and everyone laughed.

But a month later, when it was discovered that the baby had been born, everyone was shocked.

Many told her to have an abortion.

The girl repeatedly cried and said that if the child was harmed, the vampire would kill all the people in this village.

Everyone in the village was amazed when, 9 months later,

the girl gave birth to a four-legged animal from the womb.

Everyone in the maternity ward started humming in terror when they saw the four-legged animal.

 They had never seen such a strange white animal in their lives.
The girl fainted soon after giving birth.
Suddenly, he opened his eyes and sat up.

The animal also moved and sat down. He opened his eyes and looked at the people. I sniffed and searched for something.

Then the mother jumped up on the girl's lap, removed the bra, and put her face on the breast. The midwife went out of the house in fear. The rest followed him out.

There is already a lot of commotion in the house when they hear that the girl has given birth to an animal. Tensions throughout the village Suddenly, the girl came out of the house screaming like crazy.

That strange white beast in the lap. began to shout, "Beware!" Her father will annihilate the whole family if he comes to harm our child.

I can no longer be with you. I will stay in the forest from now on. No one will look for me or bother me. Defeat!

With this, the girl took the animal in her lap and ran towards the dense forest near the village.

Many people started running after him. The girl's head went bad or not! Whether it or not, who can give birth to such an animal? How did the girl get so much energy?

It started to run in the direction of the storm. After a while, the girl disappeared into the jungle. It is the evening. There is a lot of panic among the villagers about this jungle. So none of them dared go inside.

Since then, no one has seen the girl in that village. Many people would gather in the forest to fetch wood and catch birds. None of them had ever seen the girl there.

The jungle gets deeper and denser as it goes east. No one goes that way. So no one keeps track of that. The girl has no relatives to look after her. At one point, the people of the village almost forgot about the girl.

One year later, on a new moon night, the roar of a terrible beast came out of the forest. The sound was so loud that half the villagers heard it. Her heart leaped in terror at the sound. It was as if a terrible beast was blowing in anger.

From then on, the people of the houses built next to the forest could hear that terrible roar of bloodshed almost at night. The source of which is the jungle. No one would go around the forest after dusk. There was less panic during the day.

Rais Ali's house is very close to the forest. late at night. He was lying to his wife and daughter. Suddenly, he woke up to the sound of the terrible cries of cows and goats from the barn. A photo was quickly rushed there.

He went and saw a cow roaming in the yard, lying on the ground, the yard dripping with blood from the side of its throat.

Tiger or fox? No, at that moment, a strange four-legged white animal came out of the barn, doubling the size of the cow, her eyes gleaming, her lungs pounding, and she let out a terrible roar in the moonlight, looking at him! Its mouth is dripping with blood. Rais Ali left after Da Ta.
He panicked, backed away, and collided with his feet in the yard. The strange, terrible beast is preparing to jump.

Rais Ali realized that his hope of survival was over. The death of a tiger that does not come to this region is unfortunate.

What an animal! The beast jumped, but not for Rais. Gavita is holding on tight. He lifted it with great force.

He stuck it in his mouth and started running towards the forest.

In the meantime, the rest of the animals in the barn screamed in fear. People from all the nearby houses came running here.

Everyone was shocked to see blood in the yard.

Rais Mia explained the scene to everyone. Her body trembled again and again in terror as she described the body of the beast.
Everyone in the village realized that a terrible animal had entered the forest.

Almost everyone was terrified to hear its roar at night, but now it has started hunting again!

From then on, such horrible incidents started happening frequently. A terrible roar came from the forest. Occasionally, in the middle of the night, the howls of dumb animals come from the barn.

 Frightened, the owner of the house sees the terrifying white beast with Uki. He is biting and eating an animal like a madman. The rest are screaming in fear.
He can't even imagine stopping anything.

Sometimes he kills an animal from someone's house and runs towards the forest with his face. Its size seems to be increasing day by day.

It has not done any harm to people so far. However, it does not go out hunting every night. All of a sudden, after 10–15 days, it comes to the prey with a roar.
The people of the village were terrified and could not find any remedy.

I don't know if it is attacked by a group or not. Then maybe it will attack people in anger.

At least they didn't go down without explaining themselves first. Gradually, the people of the village became accustomed to the activities of this terrifying beast.

One day at 5 a.m. The sixty-year-old old lady of the village appeared walking in the morning near the forest.

The aura emitted from the sky illuminates the surrounding environment.

The purpose of the old woman is a carambola tree on the edge of the forest. In the morning it may bear fruit under it. When he reached there, he saw a handsome young man sitting on a branch of a tree.

As the old woman had no eye problems, she realized that the boy was not wearing any clothes. Such a handsome man! He looks fascinated.

In one leap, the young man came to the old woman and stood up.

The old woman could not take her eyes off him. What an enchanting face, with curly hair and black eyes, what a burning intoxication.

Seeing the young man naked like this, the old woman felt a little frustrated. The young man slowly came face to face with her. He gently touched his chin.

The old woman's whole body trembled with insanity.
Suddenly, the old woman noticed that the wrinkled skin on her body was all equal and had a soft shape; the mature hair was turning black; the pain that had been lingering in her waist had disappeared, and full youth was returning to her body. He was shocked.

He looked at himself in surprise. like a young woman of twenty-five years old. The young man turned around and started walking towards the forest. The fairy is feeling a terrible amount of excitement all over her body.

Gradually, as if obsessed, he began to follow the young man. entered the jungle. He entered this forest for the first time in his life.

However, his surprising pair of eyes are still stuck on the body of the young man. Any man can be so beautiful. Okay! White hair is coming out through the whole body of the young man.

The tail is growing from below the waist; the nails are becoming sharp and sharp! It turned into a strange white beast. It seems to the fairy that its beauty has not diminished a bit.

Like an intoxicated young woman, she continues to follow. Going deeper and deeper into the jungle
From that day on, no one in the village could find the old woman.

no one did not know where he went or what the result was!

CHAPTER 2:

The birth of a strange animal on all fours of a girl in rural life, the disappearance of the girl with her animal in the forest,

and the arrival of a terrifying carnivorous animal from that forest a year later have caused quite a stir in the village.

Everyone is in a state of panic day and night. Suddenly, one day, an old woman named Pari also went missing.

He could not be found after much searching.

No one could have guessed that the white beast was behind the disappearance of the old woman.

Then their panic would have crossed the line, and that was what was needed.

In the meantime, an exceptional incident took place in the village overnight.

One of the grandsons of Matbar Liaquat Bepari of the village lives in the town.

When he came to visit the village, he brought a large foreign dog as a gift for his grandfather.

Due to its proximity to the forest, not only in this village but also in the ten surrounding villages, there were no dogs or cats. Liaquat Ali became very interested in taming the dog.

With the arrival of a strange animal in this forest, his grandson heard from the Liaquat dealer about the hunting of village pets.

But no sound was heard of the days he was in the village. Moreover, the incident of a wild animal attack on the side of the forest did not seem unusual to him. When the holidays are over, he goes back to town.

Then one day, in the middle of the night, half the people of the village heard the roar of the white beast coming from the forest. Everyone waited in panic in their rooms.

I do not know whose house will be attacked today!
So far, as the house of the Liaquat dealer is in the middle of the village, the animals in his barn have not been attacked.
He was sleeping peacefully, his wife beside him.

There is another house near their house in which he has his daughter, daughter-in-law, and two grandchildren.

Suddenly, everyone in the house woke up with a roar. At the last moment, he heard the terrible howls of the cows in the barn. No one is left to understand what is happening.

The beast is attacking here today. Fearful, the son-in-law of Liaquat Bepari's daughter, Bakul, removed the window sill and looked outside. The barn was on one side of the yard, which was illuminated by solar lights, and his eyes were fixed on it.

Suddenly, the body became shivering. That's how a big cow is being bitten and dragged out of the barn by that terrible beast.
Bongani is coming out of the mouth. Blood is dripping. The cow is not dead yet; there is a rumbling sound coming from its throat.

The animal will be three times as big as a cow. He is trying to lift the cow by biting it well. At that moment, Tommy, the pet dog of the Liaquat dealer, came running, barking.

It is not afraid to look at the terrible beast. On the contrary, the beast was frightened and threw the prey out of its mouth. Tommy barked louder and walked towards it.

This time the animal is also blowing in anger. The sky cracked and a huge roar was heard. The blood of the murderer is dripping from his eyes.

After jumping, Tommy seems to be promising to cut off his head.

But before that, he tried to scare Tommy by shouting several times. It means he doesn't want trouble.

Tommy was not afraid. Barking, the cow and the animal came very close. The beast jumped and jumped on Tommy.

It's bigger than Tommy. However, the fastest animal is the best. Tommy jumped away at once.

At that moment, he jumped up and jumped on the back of the animal, just like a wild leopard hunts a buffalo four times bigger than him.

He wanted to put a bite on the back of the animal and scratched it evenly.

But with a flick, it knocked Tommy off his body. He jumped on Tommy again, bit his throat, and Tommy scratched his body with his toenails.

The animal growled. A rumbling sound came out of Tommy's throat. Tommy threw the beast to one side of the yard.

Tommy was lifeless for a few moments. The animal is breathing loudly. As soon as he regained consciousness, Tommy got up again, barked, and walked toward the beast.

Tommy has no energy at all. So the beast doesn't have to rush to bite Tommy this time. It let out a roar. I will jump on Tommy.

At that moment, the Liaquat dealer came out of the house with a big stick in his hand. Seeing her running like that, her daughter-in-law came out with Da in her hand.

Many of the three nearby houses hid and watched the activities of Tommy and the beast. They were shocked to see two people approaching the beast. He already had a thick stick in his hand.

This time they also came forward to shout and appeared in the yard. At that moment the beast flared up.

Disoriented, he looked back and forth. It roared a few times in a fit of rage, how many feet back and forth it roared like a raven. The people also panicked this time.

But there is no point in going backward. They are also preparing to resist if it attacks. But the beast is slowly retreating.

Once he looked at the cow after his dead prey. At that moment Tommy stood upon it. Seeing so many people, his courage and morale have increased.

His barking seemed to confuse the terrible beast. With a violent roar, it turned and ran towards the forest.

The villagers looked at each other. Pride of victory in the eyes.

I was amazed to see how fearless the courage of this one dog had awakened in them.
In an instant, their fears about the beast were halved. Liaquat leaned over and hugged Tommy.

He started shaking his head. It was in many places. She also needs care. Wagging its tail with joy, taking a deep breath, it seems to be applauding everyone.

The next morning the incident of the night spread throughout the village.
Everyone seemed to see a ray of hope during the panic.

Only dogs can tame that animal now. Not one, if necessary, they will bring hundreds of dogs to feed this village!

Several days have passed since then. The last part of the night in the village. And after half an hour the sun will rise.

Everyone in the village is asleep at this time. Just then a handsome, tall, handsome young man came out of the jungle.

Some scratch marks on the back and chest, and black eyes are burning with an intoxication.

Wearing a small shirt made of tree bark and the whole body is stupid.

Slowly he stepped away and looked around cautiously, walking towards the inside of the village.

As soon as he hears the sound of human footsteps, he turns away and walks in another direction looking for solitude.

We finally reached our destination on foot. He recognized the house. No one in the house has risen yet.

He came to the back of the house, and he left in silence. Liaquat's pet dog Tommy is lying quietly by a tree. Silently the young man came and stood behind the otter.

Tommy nodded, startled. 'Guru Gheu' became. The young man leaned over and gently touched Tommy's head. I started to caress it by turning my hand.

Tommy closed his eyes and kept sticking out his tongue, his tail dancing with him. The barking protest has stopped. The young man sat down and got a little closer to the dog. He hugged her body. Tommy's body is shaking. He has closed his eyes in devotion to the Lord.

The young man pulled out a long piece of stone from the inside of his bark. Before Tommy could understand anything, he slammed the fruit into her throat. Blood began to flow with the phoenix, and a rush of blood began to come out of Tommy's throat. The young man is holding her body tightly.

It could not move at all, even though it fluttered. Gradually his body became numb. The young man pressed Tommy's mouth with his mouth and started sucking evenly. His face began to get wet with blood.

The dog's blood is being drawn down the throat and into the stomach. After drinking the blood, he inserted the sharp fruit into the abdomen with great aggression. Suddenly the stomach split in two.

The entrails came out. This time he put his mouth there. The place seemed to bite evenly. Food is shattering with teeth.

At the end of the demonic act, he wiped his body with the skin from Tommy's body. He looked around and saw no one.

He started walking around slowly and cautiously on his way to the forest. After going some distance, I was startled.

A 16-year-old girl is walking here with a pitcher in her hand. He stared at the girl before leaving in shock.

The teenager is staring at the young man in astonishment. Only the light of dawn is shining.

He had never seen such a handsome man in his entire life.

What a strange jungle-like outfit there is after. How did you come to this village! What a sweet look, beautiful body.

The pitcher slipped from his hand. Slowly he moved closer to the boy.

What intensity is pulling him? He reached out and touched the boy's body as if trying to understand the dream. 'Who are you?'

The young man stepped back a few feet. I turned around and started running towards the forest.

He also seemed to be shocked. Teenager Sakina stared at him in astonishment.

Who is this young man?
Everyone in the village, including the Liaquat dealer, was stunned to see Tommy's dismembered body in the morning. Terrible terror filled their minds again.

CHAPTER 3:

The people of the village were stunned to see Tommy's horrible, horrible dismembered body found in the house of the best Liaquat dealer.

I don't know what the feeling was swallowing them.

The beast always roars and enters the village, hunting for its existence. But last night they did not hear any roar or attack any other animal. What revenge to kill Tommy!

What could be an animal so careful! No
one in the house heard Tommy's barking
or screaming. Nothing enters the head
except panic inside someone.
The people of Liaquat's family were the
most frightened.

I don't know if it attacked the people of
this house any other night in the anger of
that night! It doesn't occur to anyone that a
person can do such a horrible thing.

Sakina, a girl from the village, does not
know about the death of the dog. But again
and again, the face of the handsome young
man floated in his imagination.

Many villagers move to distant villages.
Looking for dogs. Wherever the dog finds
a pet, he adapts it and brings them to this
village.

At least they knew in that look that the
beast had a dog fear, and the dog became
very brave when he saw the beast. How
many dogs will it kill?

So being close to a dog gives them a lot of courage.

Hundreds of dogs were brought across the village. The Liaquat dealer's house is at 6 o'clock!

A deep part of the forest. Even if you make a mistake, no human foot is worn here. A huge hole is seen at the base of a tall, thick, leafless, tall, thick tree.

Walking through this path of holes, one can see another, unfamiliar world. Will take you to a different kingdom. Where people say nothing.

What a squeaky sound came out of it. At that moment a naked young man came out from inside.

Now it's a hot afternoon in the sunlight.

The trees are not dense here and the few trees that are there do not have enough stalks or leaves to block the entry of light.

Yet for some reason the transparent light does not reach here.

The place is surrounded by a kind of darkness even during the day.

Coming out of the hole, the young man turned around and looked up at the huge tree. Her chest trembled with terror.

Fear is all over the mind. He knows it is no ordinary tree. The tree will wake up in the evening.

The question will plague him. What will he explain! He can't do anything as he says.

The dead bodies of two women are lying in the hole with the roots of the tree.

We know both of them, the girl who gave birth to an animal a year ago, and the young man's mother.

The day he took refuge here, he fled from the locality and died on the same day due to the influence of some evil force.

That evil force also takes the responsibility of raising the animal.

That means this tree is a vampire. The body of an old woman in another village. A few days ago,

he brought her to this forest covered with fascination. However, the bodies of the two bodies did not show any slight decomposition. Nothing falls into this pit.

Only two women are not satisfied with the body of the vampire.

The monster told the young man that there must be hundreds of women's bodies in this hole.

Only then will the monster regain all its power.

And goals will be met. But he is not able
to hunt his food properly and the target of
hundreds of women is far away.
The work has to be done slowly.

Once the people of the village realize that
this animal is responsible for the
disappearance of the women in the village,
then they will be alert.

As a result, he can't bring hundreds of
women here alone. And if he can't do that,
a terrible punishment will come down
from the demonic monster.

From his inner beast-man will take away
the ability to be beast from man which at
the same time gave him the intelligence
and agility of man.

Maybe when the demon realizes it won't
work with him.
Then kill him. And he will take another
woman from the village and give birth to
another child inside her and achieve his
goal with her.

he is the child of that monster-shaped vampire tree!

When the sun went down, this part of the forest became more of a reservoir.

In the forest, first, a gentle breeze started and then the speed increased.

All the surrounding trees began to shake.

The young man was in the hole. Came out of there.

His body gradually became furry, his nails pointed, and he was transformed into a huge white beast.

The huge tree in front of him started moving terribly.

He looked back in panic. The bark of the tree began to fall off, and an ugly body of huge size came out of it.

The body is full of black sores, it is swollen like a wound, pus is accumulating in some places, and the flesh is falling away from the decay,

if you look closely, you can understand that thousands of carnivorous insects are chirping all over its body, these are its muscles and cells.

In a few moments, the gigantic tree turned into a terrifying monster-shaped headless vampire.

Insects that were buzzing on the stomach of the vampire began to move to one side. There appeared two small eyes and a large face.

The animal's body trembled in terror at the sight.

This is the powerful vampire man, whose power one day no one in the world had the power to evade! A terrible roar came out of the demon's mouth.

Looking at the animal, his eyes became a little violent, then Fu gave loudly. The animal tumbled in the air and retreated a lot.

The vampire laughed out loud, 'You're just getting bigger, you can't stand the wind! You are my most useless son.

You have not been able to guess your ability so far, you can not handle the work using your skills, and intelligence!

Failed to meet the goal! Look at your brothers once, you will know about yourself! '

All the branches and leafless trees in the vicinity trembled, and the beast looked around in terror.

It is as if many monsters are trying to get out of the bark and shells of the trees. But there is no obstacle.
The demonic murmur is coming from those trees.

The giant vampire roared again. Feeling the animal move a little closer, he felt helpless.

Began to fidget. His face became distorted.

Insects in the body are born to rot their flesh and enter the skin as soon as they eat its flesh. Its pain is also evident on its face.

It screamed, 'You see the pain of your father, the pain of your brothers!

We are getting the fruits of the evil deeds of the people of that world, our control is now in their hands.

The deception of one woman has caused us this misery, now the abandonment of hundreds of women will resurrect us. You seek the identity of your power.

Free fathers and brothers. Find out the power of the father who made you so strong in one year.

Do not deviate from the goal. Come forward to me.

The beast shrunk in fear and slowly approached the vicious demon.

The vampire's face became monstrous, all the insects in its body were running away and filling the monstrous mouth.

The vampire was chewing as if they had accumulated their juice in their mouths, and the environment was heavy with an awful horrible smell.

The demon vomited all the juice that had accumulated in his mouth and poured it on the animal.

As the man staggered when the acid fell, the animal staggered back and forth, fell to the ground, and began to stagger, whispering, an average sound coming out of its throat.

The eyes and face disappeared from the belly of the demon man, and the bark rose from the ground and covered his whole body again, it stopped its movement.

It has now been transformed into a gigantic branch-leafless, leafless tree.

The animal moved slowly and sat up. There is not a drop of vomit left in his body.

They pierced the hair and skin and went deep into his body.

The beast noticed that its shape and strength had increased more than before. Leaving a roar, he ran towards the village.

He will have to satisfy his hunger first and then he will think of doing as the demon commands.

He doesn't like it at all. But it seems that he has a role to play in fulfilling his father's goals.

CHAPTER 4:

Midnight in the village. At this time, everyone is asleep as usual.
Only occasionally can you hear the barking of a few dogs.

Since the number of dogs kept in the village is now more than a hundred.

At that moment, a huge roar came out of the jungle.

Anyone who has heard that sound knows how much this sound can shake the soul.
As soon as the animal's roar was heard, all the dogs barked together from different places. 'Well!'

The call came out like a fox from a few places. The dogs are excited.

The sound of their barking is increasing. The dogs are staring at each other, their breathing speed and chest-pounding are increasing, and their tails are dancing in the same rhythm.

The biggest dog in the village is in Liaquat's house. It raises its head and says 'Kuuuuuu!' Uttered a sound.

After that, he came out running towards the end of the village, towards the forest.

Responding to his call, all the dogs in the village ran after him.

Hundreds of dogs have gathered at the end of the village. Running here and there in excitement.

It seems that excitement is spreading among them by barking.

The people of the village also hid in fear to see what was happening, everyone has weapons and sticks for self-defense.

Although he knows that if the animal attacks, it will not be of any use. Let's see what the beast does with so many dogs!

The beast came out of the jungle leaving a bloodless roar.

In the light of the light moon, its size now seems much larger than before.

About 4 adult cows will be equal.

How the dogs lost their way when they saw the strange white beast. Aiming at the beast with all his might in his throat, 'Bark, bark!' Is doing.

Seeing so many dogs together, how the animal got frightened. But it is feeling full vigor. The animal began to move forward, roaring.

The biggest of the dogs came to the front. It is also roaring for the animal.

The animal jumped on the dog with great speed, in one leap it bit the soft part of its throat, and gradually its teeth were sinking into the soft flesh.

Suddenly he separated his head from his body.

The big dog's throat is bleeding profusely at once, its head has fallen off.

The rest of the dogs saw it and suddenly died. The atmosphere remained stagnant for a few moments.

That too let out a roar. He is running fast from side to side. They are bleeding with a sore throat.

He is taking a bath in that blood.

He is hitting their heads evenly with his four legs, scratching them with sharp nails, and tearing their eyes and mouths, preventing the injury with his huge body.

The dogs are trying to bite into his huge body.

As soon as it rises in the body, its body is falling with the speed of sweeping, the body of the animal is impossibly slippery.

After biting it, some dogs died due to the pressure on its body. They can put some pickles on the animal.

The beast once became tired of stopping their attacks and killing them.

Its white body has long since turned red with the blood of dead dogs. Seeing the dead dogs, the rest of the dogs should be scared.

But on the contrary, they are getting angrier and angrier, they have to take revenge for killing their people!

The beast killed more than fifty dogs after an hour-long battle.

Now he is angry, he understands and nothing is possible for him.

His strength has diminished a lot.

But the speed of the rest of the dogs seems to be increasing.

Now it is better to flee to the forest without hunting.

He turned around and looked at the forest. The body was exhausted.

The whole forest seemed to be mocking him.

That vampire man and his
children all look at him with sneering eyes.

They will abandon the dog they ate and
return to the forest, they will no longer
accept him as a child of the forest. Going
back means death.

This feeling turned the animal's mind
upside down, a terrible body-shaking roar
came out of its throat, and the ground and
the trees began to tremble.

He promised to destroy this village today.
Blood is rushing all over her body.

At this opportunity of its distraction, a
black dog jumped on it,

jumped on its back, and bit the torso of the animal right near the neck, the sharp teeth of the dog penetrated the flesh through the skin, and another dog jumped from behind and went under its feet.

He jumped and bit her testicles. Terrible, horrible screams came out of the beast's voice.

As soon as the body is shaken, its legs, tail, and one dog after another are jumping on purpose, biting various parts of the body, it will tear the animal to pieces.

It has lost the power to stop the attack due to the pain.

Dogs have also become dangerous. The animal tilted to the ground. The ground shook.

The dust had blown away the atmosphere here long ago. The beast looked around again, all the energy of the body was exhausted.

The dogs are biting incessantly, unable to move, just barking.

Realizing that he had reached the end of his life, he saw the flames of many burning fires coming from the side of the village, his body became completely numb, and his eyes were closed.

It was inconceivable to the people of the village that this ferocious, monster-shaped beast of the forest would be so frightened to see a dog, that the dogs would come together in groups to resist it so vigorously.

But they have long since forgotten the one thing that wild animals have feared most for thousands of years.
Fire! Nothing could be more terrifying for a wild animal.

The people of the village were watching the conflict between the immense courage of the dogs and the terrifying power of the beast, who had been hiding behind them for a long time.

At one point everyone decided that not only the spectators watching the joke,

but they would also help the dogs to kill
the animal.

Everyone was waiting for the beast to light
a torch to scare them.

Torches in one hand and weapons and
sticks in the other.

They are shouting and talking to each
other, realizing that everyone has to finish
it today, otherwise they will not get
another chance.
All the trouble is over if you can cut its
throat with a sharp weapon.

The excitement of the dogs was lessened
by the sight of the people, and they slowly
began to move away from the injured
animal.

At that moment a huge roar came from inside the forest. The whole jungle is trembling with rage.

The villagers were shocked, the beast was lying there, then where did the scream come from.
And they had never heard such a roar before.

So is there any other family of this animal in the forest? Defeat then!

When another beast came to rescue it, it was all over! Defeat!

The ground shook like an earthquake.

The soil in some places is trembling abnormally. The soil above is crumbling.

The people started running towards the village, shouting torches and weapons.
Something terrible will happen now!
That's what happened!
The dogs were frightened, staring in amazement.

They think of escaping, but they can't get the sound out even if they try with their throats. Their bodies are shaking with the ground.

The roots of a tree came out of the ground, another by its side, another by its side, so much so that the roots of the ground began to giggle around, the black crumbs of them, the colors of them, running like snakes from side to side, the heads of all of them were pointed.

This was the first time that fear and panic had appeared on the faces of the dogs. The roots began to run, aiming at the dogs. The head of a nearby dog pierced the throat of a nearby dog and its belly came out. Its body was torn apart.

The head of another root entered through the stomach and came out with the back of another dog,

the inside of the mouth of a dog came out through the mouth and came out through the belly, their body is becoming abhor-for.

The ground is dripping with blood, the stomach is bursting and the entrails are coming out.

They tried to run away but their bodies twisted their legs. Then he pulled the body from two sides and tore it in two.

Within minutes, all the dogs' dismembered bodies were left behind. None of the villagers looked back to see the scene, one ran to his house and closed the door, trembling with fear.

Sweat dripping from their bodies smells of unwelcome danger. What happened? What will happen now!

In the open wilderness, there are now hundreds of dead dogs with their mutilated body parts, and the gnawing roots are scurrying about, whose father is not a real tree.

One vampire male. The terrified animal moved a little, then found the source of some energy remaining in the body.
It jumped up and stood up. I was shocked to see this strange sight all around.

The vampire man saved him! He has to pay for it. Her whole body is burning with pain, her head is spinning.

The beast began to run. Everything looks blurry in the eyes.

He should go back to the forest. But he is running towards the inside of the village.

Whether he is running around in pain by mistake or running for revenge in a fit of rage, cannot be guessed by the speed of his run.

Teenager Sakina is fast asleep in the bed of the house. At the far end of this village is their home, far away from the jungle. So no word of the disturbance has reached their house so far.

He has no idea what is going on there. Suddenly, his chest trembled at the sound of something heavy falling behind his house.

He got up and sat on the bed. From the next room, his blind father growled in terror, 'Who? Who?

What happened Ray! ' Sakina said, 'I think the tree is breaking!' A tree fell halfway down the back of the house for many days. Still, as he was leaving the house, he suddenly felt a kind of fear.

He had heard from the villagers about a terrible beast. He came out slowly with Da in one hand and Hurricane in the other. Going to the back of the house, I was startled.

A man is unconscious, has no clothes to wear, and his whole body is soaked in blood. Going a little closer, I recognized the young man.

This is the beautiful young man he saw that morning. His body trembled at the pool. Slowly proceeded to the young man. Trying to understand what is happening!

CHAPTER 5:

Sakina is stunned and leans toward the naked young man. The whole body of the young man is covered in blood.

Signs of injuries are also evident in various parts of the body. Seeing the man's chest rising and falling, he realized that he was still alive.

He looked around and saw no one.

What people will he call! Suddenly he looked at the young man's face and felt a kind of Maya. He was not fascinated by such looks at this age.

After seeing the young man that morning, he saw only this face in his dreams and imagination for many nights.

Now he wants to get closer and heal himself by serving him.

Maybe the boy will be grateful to her for the rest of his life. How much more can happen! But the man is so big that he can't take her home.

Still, he tried to raise his head with one hand behind the man's head. The young man suddenly moved, blinking.

Sakina's heart is pounding. Realizing that the man wanted to stand with the weight in his hand, he pressed his shoulder tightly behind him.

With the efforts of the young man and his two, both were able to stand. Half the mass of the man fell on Sakina's body and Sakina's legs became numb and she could not walk.

The man has no complete knowledge. Yet slowly the energy seemed to return to the young man's body.

He put a little weight on Sakina's body and started walking on his strength as if he was drowsy.

Sakina realized that if she took the man to her house, her father would ask various questions.

Just as little boys and girls pick up a valuable toy and hide it in a box without telling anyone, the young man seems to be his own thing, just as one can claim it as his own when he sees it.

Even if no one knows about this man, the young man will be separated from him.

Someone will take it away. Feel we have 'Run out of gas' emotionally and emotionally.

There is an abandoned house opposite their house. When my father's eyes were good, various agricultural implements were kept in that house. He took the man into the room and laid him on the floor. Quickly he got out and went to his father's house. Dad was still anxious to know what the sound was.

Sakina mumbled and said that the tree had collapsed. When the father fell asleep, he reached the man's house again with his father's lungi. Bringing buckets and mugs, he wiped the man's body with a towel, wiped his blood, and vomited, but still began to clean.

Then he put on his cloth. Shocked, he noticed that the wounds on the man's body were healing on their own. He brought a sheet and pillow from his house and arranged the bed for the man as much as he could. I do not know what to do.

The man's knowledge has not yet returned. He can't be with the man all night.

Sakina doesn't get any leisure from her father since her father lost his eyesight.

After a while, he woke up and became anxious to hear Sakina's voice. With some hesitation, he locked the room from outside and went to his room, and lay down. After fidgeting for a long time, he fell asleep at one stage.

When he woke up, he got up and got out of bed. I remembered the man from last night.

What happened in the dream! He looked at his shirt and shrugged. There is blood everywhere.

He went to the next room and saw his father still sleeping.

He changed his clothes and went out and stood outside the locked room.

When I opened the lock and went inside, it seemed again and again that I would see nothing inside.

But no, that's the handsome human figure lying on the sheet. In the light of day, her beauty seems to have increased a thousand times.

Any man is so beautiful! In a way, he used to listen to fairy tales as a child. The boy is a prince, lost his way and came here!

Seeing the man now seems to be perfectly healthy. The man blinked and wanted to open his eyes. Sakina's chest is throbbing. A sweet voice came out of the young man's voice, 'Who are you? Why am I here? '

Sakina calmed down a bit and replied, 'You fell unconscious in the back of my house last night. I'll clean your body and bring it here. Who are you Where is your home?

The boy's head trembled with pain.
Holding his head with both hands, he said,
'Yes, I remember everything.

I live in a village on the other side of the
forest. I went to the forest to cut wood.

But one day I lost my way while walking
inside. As evening falls, I am suddenly
confronted by a strange white beast.

It attacks me. I beat him with an ax.

Then I kept running like crazy. It still
follows me. Maybe I came here on the run.
'

'But I saw you one morning before!'
'Me! This is the first time I've been here! '
'Maybe! But ... whatever!
Sakina's face turned red with shame.

She is like the beautiful daughter of a poor
woodcutter in a fairy tale, a prince who
has lost his way has come to her. The
young man suddenly said, 'Not me, I'm
very hungry!'

Sakina also remembered her father's words. Babaoto will want food a little later.

She said to the young man in a sweet voice full of shame so that he would not make any noise and would not go out. It would be dangerous for people to see him here. After a while, he will come and go with food.

The young man, as a child, simply said that whatever he said would happen, and he would not go anywhere. Then he left the house to prepare food.

The villagers hid in the house all night in a panic. No one could fathom the horrific scene of the dogs fighting with the beast last night.

But then what happened! They saw an earthquake and thought that the whole village would be submerged.
Some more terrifying beasts will come running from the jungle.

Some more terrifying beasts will come running from the jungle. When nothing like that happened, they left Huff alive.

Frightened in the morning, some people reached the end of the village.

He was surprised to see that there was not the slightest sign of last night's violence anywhere in the desert.

The whole place is covered with silence. There is not a drop of blood or dead dogs here.

They don't even know what happened to the big beast. Excitement and panic are engulfing them now in fear of the unknown.

Who cleaned everything, how did that happen! The night will descend again in this village.

No one knows what danger awaits the villagers.

Then about seven days passed. The villagers could not hear the roar of the beast from the forest, nor did they see any sign of its presence.
Their lives gradually returned to normal.

Surprisingly, for the past seven days, no one but Sakina has known that an unknown young man has been living in a room in Sakina's house.

Not even his blind father Hossain Mia.

The young man never leaves the house. Sakina only goes to the house three times to feed the man. People in the neighborhood do not come to their houses.

Some of Sakina's girlfriends used to chase her away to meet her. When they see the young man, they will all want to take him home.

She just wants to be alone with the guy all the time. As soon as his father sleeps at night, he goes to the man's house.

The two talked almost all night. Hear the story of his life from the man. Tell your own story.

The man listens to her with great interest as he listens to the life of his village, the people of the village, why they don't want to go to the forest, wants to know their fears, and discusses what fascinates them most.

Sakina once asked the man if it would be okay to stay here so long, that he will not go back to your house! The young man said that his body looked fine on the outside but very weak on the inside.

The day will come when he will be completely healed. And he doesn't want to leave Sakina. Sakina appreciates the food.

Sakina blushed in embarrassment.
The young man added that if he wanted to return to his village, he would have to walk through the jungle for about one day and one night.

He will leave on the date of the next full moon if Sakina lets him go.

And he said that he would not tell to anyone in the village because the people of the village believe that the village on the other side of the forest is inhabited by vampires.

Everyone can harm him thinking he is a vampire. Sakina never told anyone. That's the way it goes.
Another week passed.

One day the young man asked Sakina, how did your father's eyes become blind?

Sakina said that Hossain Mia was working in the field one day. At that time some insects got into his eyes.

His eyes start to burn. He comes home. Within a few hours, the eyes became swollen. A lot of herbal medicine and scrubbing did not work.

The eyes remained swollen for three days. Then the swelling gradually subsided. But Hossain Mia's eyes never came back.

Apart from Hossain Mia, Sakina has no other relatives left in the world. The story of the death of his mother and younger brother told him.

Seeing the young man's face, it was understood that the young man was in pain after hearing the words.

Then he smiled and said, I know a way to make your father's eyes better.

Sakina almost jumped up. The young man said that there was a big, powerful tree in that forest that could not do any impossible work.

There is medicine for all diseases in its roots. If he gives a little juice from the roots of that tree to his father's eyes, he will be completely healed.

Sakina didn't want to believe it at first. But the young man began to say how many people in his village he had seen with his own eyes.

What the power of the tree!

If you want not only medicine for the disease but also for that tree, you can make people dhoni with wealth right away.

At first, he disbelieved, but gradually he thought that the man was telling the truth.

There are so many strange things in the forest. No one could have imagined that such a strange white animal could live in that forest.

The young man told him that he knew that tree in the forest. It is possible to go there in one night and bring the roots.

Today is full moon night, Sakina can take him to that tree if she wants.

Sakina remained after the conflict, the man assured her a lot.

Dad is happy to see her again.

No one in the village will know about their departure. Sakina decided to go to the forest tonight with this young man to gather roots.

Almost all the people of the village including Hossain Mia are asleep at midnight.

In the twinkling of an eye, Sakina followed the young man into the deep forest.

CHAPTER 6:

When the village fell asleep in the middle of the night, Sakina entered the deep forest with a stranger in the moonlight. Hopefully, if the man can find the tree, his father will probably be able to regain his sight.

At least for the last two weeks, she has realized that she will not be harmed if she stays with him. The two of them walked silently for a long time.

At the beginning of the forest, there is less difficulty in walking as there are few trees and shrubs.

However, he did not notice that the young man's face became a little stiff as soon as he entered the forest, the muscles of the body were getting stronger and the density of hair follicles was also increasing.

Sakina was just walking around the forest with fascinated eyes. The jungle that is so beautiful and scary from the inside cannot be understood from the outside.

The cries of various animals are coming from all over the forest. They do not sleep at night!
The sound of crickets, the rustling of feet, and the walk with a handsome young man thrilled his mind.

Sakina is sure that if this young man had not been with her, she would have run out of the jungle in fear.

After walking a long way, I thought, where are they going? Is there a tree whose root sap can restore sight to humans?

How strange the man looks in the soft light of the moon. Why he did not notice so much hair on his body for so long! The man a few steps ahead of her, Sakina wants to touch his body.

Suddenly the young man went to the base of a tree and sat down.
Sakina looked at the tree in surprise and saw that it was a very small tree, not matching the description given by the man.

The young man looked at him and smiled, 'It's not that tree, it's deep inside. If you're tired, get some rest. ' He was really tired. He also sat down next to her.

The young man is looking at her, what a strangely beautiful man. As the young man's body is trembling, Sakina seems to have some illusion in his eyes.

The man's eyes are turning red, his body hair is getting thicker.

How is this possible? The man came a little closer to her and grabbed her by both hands. Said, 'The rest of the way you have to go alone.

You will continue to walk straight along this side. There can be a danger if two people walk side by side here.

I will walk behind you behind that bush. Neither of them will say anything. Come on!

With this, the man quickly ran and went behind the bushes.
Sakina was shocked. He was not ready for it at all. What will he do alone?

What a danger if the two go together! Looking at the road ahead, the vibration of the book increased. Dense bushes, thick rows of trees.

He called the man several times. Didn't get a response. Then he started walking towards the front in fear.

The light of the jotsna that is entering through the gap of the tree can somehow make its way.

Huge bushes to his right. The rustling sound of someone else's way is being heard from his side.

In other words, the young man is walking beside him. But the footsteps seem so heavy that a four-legged animal is walking, whispering how the man is breathing so loudly!

He walked alone for about an hour with the fear of granulation.

The body is numb with fatigue, but he does not know if it will stop.

Meanwhile, the trees are fewer. But that bush still separates the young man from her. He is walking fast and his mind is fidgeting.

What I do know is that the smell of danger is hitting my nose. Large bush to his right. Or there are some small bushes on the side.

As soon as he saw it for a moment, a stream of ice-cold air flowed down his spine.

A pair of twinkling eyes stared at him from behind the bushes. There is no doubt that it is a wild animal.

Another pair of eyes came out from that side, another pair from that side. At that moment, three terrifying tigers jumped out of the bushes. The roar was aimed at Sakina.

He no longer has the strength to run backward. He just addressed the man and said, 'Save me!'

A tiger jumped at him, screamed with his mouth, covered his head with both hands, closed his eyes, and sat down on the ground. Preparation for death.

But no, that didn't hurt him. He opened his eyes and saw a huge white animal biting the tiger's trunk.

He threw the tiger away with his mouth. Another tiger let out a roar and jumped on the animal. The beast struck him on the stomach with its head, and as soon as it fell to the ground, it grabbed its body with both feet. He also lost consciousness.

The third animal is a much smaller tiger than these.

Seeing the fighting ability of the beast, he glanced at his prey once. Then he started running in the opposite direction.

The beast turned and looked at Sakina. He realizes that the beast saved him from the tigers, but not for any great purpose.

This fight is just to make the victim of others his food. He had never heard the name of such a strange carnivorous animal in his life. But the beast showed no signs of jumping on him.

It turned upside down and sat on its knees. There was a slight rumble in his mouth. He gestured to Sakina with his head and told her to get on his back. Sakina looked around in fear.

The young man is nowhere to be seen, what a danger he has! He called the young man a few times, but no one answered from the side of the bush.

The beast looked at him with a crooked nose, as if something funny was happening! Sakina slowly went and got on the animal's back. He held it tightly so that its fur would not fall off.

Everything seems like a dream to him. Nothing that is happening to him can happen in reality.

How could such a huge beast be pulling her so close, Sakina thought for a moment that if she was with this beast there would be no more danger for her. Of course, how is his mind for the young man, where is he!

The animal ran with him on its back, crossing the bushes, crossing various holes and high slopes.

After about half an hour, the beast brought him under a huge tree. He stared at the tree with astonished eyes.

Such a big tree, but the tree has no leaves, the bark is also a strange color.

There is a hut at the beginning. The beast dropped him from the back and threw him to the ground.

Then he ran away and disappeared into the forest. Stunned, a teenage girl stood in this terrifyingly beautiful nature.

There was only surprise, wailing, and panic in his eyes.

After a few moments, he heard someone's footsteps behind him and looked around. The young man is standing there.

He hurried to the man and said, 'Where have you been? I thought there was a big danger. A strange beast has brought me this far.

'I was following you secretly according to the rules of the jungle. Suddenly I was shocked to see the tigers.

That's when I saw that animal saved you. I never saw him again.

Maybe the animal would see me and attack me. I came here after you.

The beast came running at me so fast, how did you get here on foot, at the same time?'
'I've come to the shortcut road.

'Then why didn't you take me to the shortcut road?'
'Ah! You look so picky. Take a good look at the tree.

As soon as I looked at the tree, the fear came back. In front of him, he seems to be a small, helpless man. At any moment the tree seems to move.

Sakina pointed to the hole in the tree's ankle and asked, 'What's there?' The young man was surprised and said, 'I don't understand either. Will you go inside it?

Sakina was shocked, 'Never! What a horror!

'Then kneel and close your eyes to the tree and pray from the heart. Say, Lord, fulfill my heart's desire.

Sakina moved a little closer to the tree in fear. Sitting on his knees, he closed his eyes and muttered, 'Yes, Lord, mighty tree, restore my father's sight.

The young man is standing close to his neck. Her eyes are shining. As if to jump at any moment to bite Sakina's neck.

Sakina opened her eyes and looked back, the young man controlled himself.

He held Sakina by the hand and made her stand. Taken behind a huge tree. The hand gestures showed a few young roots. Sakina picked them up.

The young man said in a serious voice, 'If you put its juice in your father's eyes, he will see it again.

Sakina's mind danced with joy. Can't believe the moment. The young man said, 'Towards the end of the night.

The beast that has brought you so far is the offspring of this tree. Slave of the tree. The tree loved you and sent the beast to save you.

I believe the beast will come here as soon as I go into hiding. He will take you to the village.

Excited, Sakina said, 'And you?'
'I'll run the short way.

We will meet again at the end of the forest. The beast does not like men. It would be dangerous to see me. I went.

Saying this, the man left the girl alone again and went into the forest.

Surprisingly for Sakina! The strangely large white beast appeared a moment later along the path by which the young man had disappeared.

He knelt and motioned for her to get up on his back.

Sakina got on the animal's back. He hugged her tightly. The hunters have kept the git near the waist.

The beast began to run through the forest with the speed of the wind.
The beast stopped at the end of the forest.

The village can be seen. Sakina fell from her back. Once the beast looked at Sakina, then instantly turned around and ran into the forest.

Shortly after that, the handsome young man came out from behind. Nothing got into Sakina's head as to how the man got away so quickly.

The young man is standing in front of her. Sakina's chin touched his hand, 'I have to say goodbye this time.'
Sakina said in surprise, 'I mean!'

'You have done so much for me.

I will always be grateful to you. But I also have to go back to my home. I think this is a beautiful time. '

The girl's eyes got wet. Can't find what to say.

The young man said, 'The night is almost over. You go home.

We will meet again. This medicine will cure your father. But you have to pay the price for the tree.

What! What's the price? Why didn't you tell me earlier?

'Don't be afraid. When your father regains his sight, everyone will want to know how it happened!

You will then tell the truth to everyone, preaching the importance of the powerful tree to everyone in the village.

And with any help from them, the tree in danger has the power to benefit them.

So they come to the tree and present their needs. But no man should enter this forest.

Only women come in groups to pray to the tree.

Because men are unnecessary in that area. If necessary, you will guide them. Just don't say that you've met me.

'If you hear that, almost all the women of the village will go to that tree and appear. I have already told you that there is no end to their problems.

'That's what we want!'
'You mean?'
'Nothing. You must tell them to go there at night.

They will not find the tree in daylight. But you have to do your job. Tell me? '
'I will.

Go, then. See you again.
The man slowly went into the woods.
Sakina's mind is trembling with an evil
fear.

The mind is filled with sadness because
the man has left. Towards the end of the
night, he set off slowly, on his way home
with a worried mind.

CHAPTER 7:

The teenage girl spent a beautiful night in
the deep forest. The body is now numb
with fatigue. The mind is still restless until
the juice of the prey returns to the sight of
the father, he will not find any peace in the
mind.

He must be examined to see how true the
words of that unknown young man are,
how far the power of that huge tree
extends, true! The light of dawn is shining
all around. Sakina has reached home.

Frightened, he entered the house, saw his father asleep, and left the hop alive.
No one knew about his campaign. He vowed not to tell anyone about this night in the jungle if the root medicine did not work.

He cut the prey almost like a mash. Slowly he came and sat on the bed next to his father's head. Bharata's coating began to spread over her closed eyes.

Her father was shocked, 'Who? Who? ' Says. Sakina calmed him down. Said, 'I'm giving you a medicine, Dad, you can see again from now on.' Hossain Mia smiled, '

Sakina is upset! What a dead thing to live again! What time is it? The mother fell asleep. '
'Oh Dad, lie down quietly.

He left the house with the coating. Chest throbbing. What will happen now! Once it seemed that everything is human, or it happens again!

At the last moment, he thought, what happened to him at night, then what a surprise when his father regained his sight due to the effect of miraculous power!

The outside has become completely fair. Sakina is sitting quietly in the yard to get a seat, I think a thousand fears.

Suddenly a father's cry came from the house. Mind you! It seems that the father is crying with joy! He ran home. Hossain Mia almost jumped out of bed.

He staggered and hugged Sakina, 'Murray! How many days later did I see my mother's face. Look, I'm watching!

What medicine did you give! ' Sakina also started crying with joy.

All true then! The young man was filled with gratitude for the huge tree.
Leaving his daughter, Hossain Mia ran towards the village road.

He couldn't believe it, he could see again. He ran around the whole village like a child. How long after watching these beautiful scenes! All the people of the village were surprised to see Hossain Mia.

How did the man regain his sight? Hossain Mia started telling everyone that Sakina had applied for a strange medicine in his eyes, that is what brought back his light.

Slowly the rumor of Hossain Mia's miraculous regaining his sight spread throughout the village.

Everyone came to Hossain Mia's house and gathered a crowd. Sakina said, suddenly she gets a dream order to go to the forest.

According to the path found in the dream, he appears under a big tree at night. Hatumure prays to the tree with the father. The tree helps him find his roots, and his father regains his sight.

The people of the village listened in amazement. Many believe the incident. Some say again, crazy delirium.

Hossain Mia has recovered on his own. Does the tree fulfill the wish again?

Sakina tells them that there is nothing in the world that the tree cannot give. But that part of the forest is dangerous for men.

Only women can go there and have to go at midnight. Pray to the tree in Hatumure.

The incident spread throughout the village.

None of the villagers ever went deep into the jungle.

There was no need to go. Many people knew that there was a big river at the end of this forest which merged with the sea.

Those who are very old also heard from their elders in their childhood that an ancient group used to live on the bank of that river at the end of the forest. They were worshipers of various demon gods.

They used to worship the terrible demons. He used to invite them and bring them among them. With their help, they would fulfill their desires. Gained, longevity, and infinite strength. People from far and wide used to come and offer sacrifices to the demons.

After being tricked by an anti-vampire woman, the group's chief Matbar later neglected to worship a powerful vampire. The demon, in a fit of rage, cursed all the children, including the village head. Cursed are the trees for eternity. The rest of the group could not escape his anger.

An unknown strange disease spread among the rest of the group. Insects begin to grow inside their bodies. They are absorbed by the blood and swell in shape.

Then gradually the number becomes a few thousand inside the body. Human flesh comes out through holes. It is scattered all over the body.

Thousands of holes are made all over the body, from which the pus comes out fluently and the insects are busy getting in and out through the path.

There are sores on the body, there is a foul odor all around, and their flesh is swallowed and falls from the body.

Became horrible all around. Only a few were able to escape then.

Everyone in the village listened to these words as stories.

That was too many, many years ago. There was nothing to believe. Some of the fugitives had taken refuge in nearby villages.
These stories have spread from them.

Realizing the terrible dangers that vampire practice brings, they stay away from it in later life. After that these stories were almost forgotten by the villagers till today.

Sakina's father's vision was restored, Sakina's jungle story was told, and the village elders were moved to remember the story of that childhood.

He said that when they were young, they heard about such trees from adults. The tree is a vampire's curse.

That is the vampire tree. Trapping small benefits will do great harm. So that no one goes to the forest after greed even if he makes a mistake. No one understands the significance of the old man's words.

The villagers are superstitious but not familiar with the vampire thing. However, there was an atmosphere of peace and tranquility in the village. Because the white beast had a terrible fight with the dogs that night, and they never saw it again. So much of the panic was gone.

Some young men in the village became curious about Sakina's description.

If there is a tree that will fulfill all the desires of their minds! They entered the forest in broad daylight in groups to find the tree.

But as soon as he entered the deepest part of the forest, he lost his way and started to face the wild animals.

Somehow they managed to escape from the jungle with their lives.

Do not dare to enter the forest again. Like Sakina's path, many men wanted to go deep into the forest at night and reach the tree.

But they lost their way a little further and had to return home with great difficulty. No one has dared to raise women yet. Where men can't, how can they enter the forest at midnight!

One day a woman came to Sakina and listened to all the details. The woman was childless. Reached the end of his youth. Now living and dying are not a big deal for him.

Fearless mind. So one night he dared to hide and entered the forest with a hurricane in his hand. I started walking straight. At that time a road was seen in the forest.

It's as if people have been walking for a long time. Walking down that path, he reached the monster-shaped tree. All the minds and souls are throbbing with fear and panic.

Hatumure prayed to a child near him. Then he went back home. There was no danger on the way.

Shortly afterward, the woman discovered that she had children. She and her husband almost went insane.

The villagers were also surprised to see this change in Phulbanu's life in his last youth. The word spread slowly.

Phulbanu went to the forest late at night. Praying to that tree is going to fulfill the hope of having children.

The women of the village became enchanted and thrilled.

That's true then! Even if no man can, the tree fulfills the desires of women!

From then on, almost at night, sometimes alone, sometimes in groups, a group of women was seen entering the forest with lights in their hands.

They find a way to reach the tree very easily as soon as they enter, they are not attacked by any animal.

Just looking at the big tree, devotion is awakened and ing in their minds. Informing their prayers to it.

Everyone's prayers are being fulfilled. Some want children, some want more crops, some want money, and some want freedom from disease.

As the days go by, the number of women in the jungle increases at night. The importance of the tree has spread far and wide in everyone's mouths.

After that, the terrible game of destiny started happening with them.

Someone entered the forest with a group of six people and suddenly one of them disappeared.

Many were found but he was not found. Neither in the forest nor the village.

The wife of one of the villagers entered the forest without informing anyone and said that she would go near the tree.

But he never returned. No one knew where he went missing.

The women disappeared at such a different time, differently, that ordinary women were not so terrified.

I thought, maybe the girls have been hunted by wild animals. If you want to get such a big help, you have to take a little risk!

But as the day wore on. The number of missing women also increased. Which is eye-catching.

Now almost all the women in the neighborhood come here every night. Most of them can go back. Only a few went missing. Where do they go?

The old vampire tree man is fascinated by his child's intellect. He did not expect it to happen so quickly.

The beast is born with half a human body. How many decades later the hopes of his mind are going to be fulfilled. The way to overcome the curse is coming very close.

There are now 60 women sleeping in his cot. And it will only take 40 victims. That handsome young man is hiding behind a tree.

So a woman is coming forward with a hurricane in her hand, there is no one else around her.
Seeing the young man, the girl stopped. The young man went behind a tree. The girl came to the tree line like a drunk. He wrapped himself around the young man's body.

At that moment, he was startled by the existence of a hairy body in his arm. He looked up and saw a white animal wrapped around him.

Before he knew it, the animal bit him on the neck. Young man, the animal thing is unclean. The beast is dragging its 61st prey woman into the hollow of the tree. From within the tree came a shout of joy. Who knows, 61 bodies have been piled up inside this hole !.

CHAPTER 8:

The bodies of 61 women were deposited in the hollow of that huge tree in the forest.

Once the hundreds are fulfilled, something will happen in the jungle that has been seeking power in this jungle for hundreds of years.

The source of that energy, the goal, no man has ever known. No one has any idea what is going to happen here.

About 100 years ago today. There was a village on the bank of the river at the end of this forest. Where about twenty families of a group lived.

Hunting in the forest, the fruits of the trees, and the vegetables produced were cutting their lives very well.

They had no separate identity from the Creator.

Who were their ancestors, since when did they live on the banks of this river, except for a few old people who knew the history, no one had such curiosity about the outside world.

They considered the jungle as their lord. They did not consider anyone but their group as their own.

They used to worship the big, strange trees that they saw in the forest.

They asked for help in times of danger and offered their food.

But after a while, they realize that the trees do not help them in their bad times or danger.

It was then that the group of people went hunting deep in the forest one day and found some horrible, terrifying idols in the hollows formed near the roots of a large tree.

Once they look at them, their chests tremble with fear. Feel they have never before experienced such a powerful force.

Who left the idols here! When they arrived in groups, the idols were taken to a forested area near their village and placed in a hidden, secret, and beautiful place.

They could not take them to their village due to some kind of fear.

Then some of the group started dreaming about these idols.

An unseen voice from behind the idols began to give them various commands and advice.

He said that for the people of the group to start worshiping idols, they would be rewarded with something they could not have imagined.

Fear and devotion still work in their minds when they look at their idols.

So quickly everyone started worshiping the vampire idols.

They began to communicate their various needs to them, seeking treatment for the dangers of the disease.

The village was filled with miraculous power.

All the problems of the people of the group began to disappear, and all the desires of their minds began to be fulfilled miraculously.

Some were attacked by wild beasts, and some went hunting every day.

The origin of wild animals began to decline.

They were then fascinated by the power of these idols. However, they have not yet fully worshiped the demon.

After that, they started getting dream orders that the people of this group have to quench their thirst and hunger for idols.

They also got instructions on how to do it. At first, he brought various animals and offered them to the idols.

Only then did they realize that they needed human blood to worship.

They became terrified thinking of themselves.
After that, they started leaving the first village.

People from other villages around the forest were trapped and brought here.

The vampires had already given various miraculous powers to the villagers.

To satisfy the greedy and powerful vampires, they go out hunting people with all their might. And offer sacrifices at the feet of their idols.

At one time they started to enjoy these. The barbarians became violent. The people of the group are getting stronger day by day.

Almost every month human sacrifices started happening here. Sometimes children, sometimes old women, teenagers, young women.
It has become a village of horrible vampire devotees.

After receiving the dream order, they pursue many more powerful demonic powers.
They make idols out of wood and clay, soak them in human blood and give fullness to the rest of the vampire idols.
There is a village on the other side of the forest.

No one could have imagined that they could be behind The forest was inaccessible and full of wild animals, so no ordinary people would come here.e disappearance of some of their people.

Almost a long time passes. One day a farmer in the forest and head lost his way after entering the forest.
Many a night of walking is spent in the forest where the villagers worship the vampire idols.

From a distance, he sees the light and hears the screams of the people. Who is doing what so many nights in the jungle!

He went there secretly and was stunned by what he saw. Huge figures A few terrifying statues. In front of them, three people are sitting on their hands and knees.

Surrounding them are some people with strange clothes, faces, and various meteorites painted on their bodies. Sharp weapon in hand.

The people sitting there are whining with intoxication. Suddenly the idols trembled. The meteorite people shouted something. Then he lowered the weapons along the necks of the people.

The body of the three was separated from the head. The people roared with joy. The man was stunned.
I turned around and started running towards the locality.

The next night he returned to the village. His condition was then terribly debilitating.

He told the villagers what he had seen in the forest. Everyone was terrified and the incident seemed unbelievable. But he died a few hours later.

After that, the rumor about the jungle spread around. But no one dared to enter the deep forest day and night to confirm the truth of the word.

At that time there was an era of complete barbarism in Pishachi village.
They do not capture more than one village, they know that once there is panic, people from all other villages will come together in one group.

Then their danger. So they hunt people from distant villages. Today, three people have been arrested.

Two men and a young woman. Tribal chief Aman came to see the people. The young woman was stunned to see the girl.

This is the first time she has seen such a beautiful girl. The girl is not wearing proper clothes.

Aman felt a strong attraction toward the girl. He said he would take the girl away for a while before the sacrifice.

No one was happy but did not bother the tribal chief. Aman is a young, new tribal chief.

Her older brother died in her sleep a month ago.
Aman tells everyone that his elder brother wanted to betray the demon gods so he was killed by a miraculous power and from now on he is the leader of that group.

His elder brother's wife, however, alleged that Aman had killed his elder brother out of greed for power. Since then, no one has been able to find his elder brother's wife and only daughter.

However, it is not possible to oppose the tribal chief.

Aman forcibly dragged the girl to his room. He takes his wife out of the house and stays in the house till late at night.

Today is the night of sacrifice. The rest of the group took the girl for sacrifice and said that he would marry her. Nothing can be sacrificed for him.

Aman himself knows that if he does not kill three people tonight, there will be a great danger from the demons.

In his greed for power, he has secretly sacrificed his elder brother's wife, daughter, and one of his opponents in this village.

He declared that there did not impede the sacrifice. Instead of this girl, he sacrificed his ex-wife for the demon.

Everyone was shocked to see Aman's cruelty. They have never publicly sacrificed their people before. This was a serious injustice in the time of Aman's elder brother. Aman's wife started crying.

That is how the sacrifice ended that night. The young girl was bewildered when she regained her life and became engrossed in Aman's entertainment.

Aman married the girl. A few months passed in the same way. The girl has also adapted to the group.

He had been living in a village with a very poor family. Here she has the honor and dignity of a queen. Everyone is afraid of him.
He succumbed to this greed. Aman has been suffering from depression lately.

It seemed to him that they were just trying to hunt people down and sacrifice the vampires at the risk of danger.
Compared to that, the vampires do them little good. Even the miraculous powers seem boring to him now.

There is no demon more powerful than that! Whose power will make him more powerful?
Not just this jungle. It will have an effect everywhere in the neighborhood.

His devotion diminishes from the vampires, often secretly searching for some great power hidden in the jungle.

CHAPTER 9:

In the mind of Aman, the leader of the demon-worshiping group, greed for a greater power was born.

He often discusses with his new wife that none of the demons they worship are omnipotent.

His wife also supports him and says that if he searches the jungle, maybe he can find a stronger force.

Which will make them the most powerful people in the whole region.

Aman continues his secret search in the jungle with some of his faithful loyalists of any power. Long cuts like this.

He does not find any new miracle. Each month, of course, three human sacrifices are offered to their vampire idols.

However, the people of all the nearby villages are now very careful. However, under the influence of the miraculous power of the demon, they do not have to get up to speed to get prey.

The river near their village is very dangerous.
So they don't go to the other side of the river, and there is no question of anyone coming from the other side.

Some of the women in the group were sitting on the river bank doing some work. At that time he was surprised to see a small boat come and crowd the river bank.

Who came with such a small boat on this fast-flowing river!

There is no boatman on the boat. A beautiful woman came down from the boat. Wearing nice sari cloth, body full of gold ornaments.

He slowly approached the women. This unfamiliar lady also knows their language.

The beautiful lady requested them to take her to Aman, the head of the group. They could not answer with their mouths.

He appeared in front of Aman's house with his wife.

Aman's wife is likely to have children, so she is currently in a different room.

Aman came out quite annoyed at the call of the girls.

He was enjoying the company of someone inside, it can be understood by looking at his dress. But when he went out, his face changed for a moment. He seemed to be stunned.

Rupavati can't take her eyes off the girl. The girl opened her mouth first, 'Aman will know my respect. I can come in!

The girls of the group left as soon as Aman winked. Once Uki was in his room, two more girls came running out of there.

You can understand who they are by looking at their clothes. Aman felt a little ashamed. Then he invited, 'Come inside.

The girl slowly entered the room. Seeing a seat, he sat down. Aman's eyes are rolling all over the girl's body. Then he leaned closer and asked, 'Who are you?

The girl replied in a shy voice, 'I heard you are looking for a great power! I am his messenger.

Aman was startled. In an instant, the fascination and gloom vanished. The wish that had been in my mind for so long vanished.

How did the girl know it! Her voice sounded a little harsh, 'I don't understand anything about you!'
'I have come here at the behest of the great power of this jungle.

He is introverted. He keeps track of your searches. He is the only one who deserves to be the lord of a dreamy group like you.

Aman went out a little and looked around to see if there was anyone.

Danger will come if anyone knows that he no longer wants to worship these demon gods.

He enters the house again and says to the girl, 'What do you want!
You are worshiping an evil force. Which is against the prevailing custom of the jungle. Which makes your hands bloody.

With a little bit of power and greed for power, you are becoming vampires.

Terrible dangers await you in the future. Long ago the ancient holy spirit of this forest killed all the evil forces in the vicinity.

He kept it locked inside the statue. You have reawakened it. So you have to destroy this demonic power again. The reign of the ancient holy power will continue here.

Aman was very upset to hear these weird theories. 'I don't think you mean so straightforwardly.

What good would it do us to worship your holy spirit, destroy this demonic force!

And how powerful is your holy spirit that we need help to destroy this evil force!

If he could do it once before, why isn't he doing it now? '
The source of energy is human devotion.

Conflict of power and energy is a terrible danger. So what people do very easily requires a huge organization to make holy energy. Anyway, it's up to you. I'm just her maid, messenger.

I will leave now. '
'How did you get here?'
'On the boat.

Surprise! Boat on this river! You wait here. You're not going anywhere. I will test the power of your holy spirit.

With this Aman left the house. Shortly after, some members of the group came and informed the girl that her boat had been wrecked by the river.

Aman tells her to stay here for the night. The girl did not realize that the man was trying to block her way. Wonder fool!

This lady, who is a stranger at best, had to stay in the hut of Aman, the head of the group. Everyone in the group became curious about the girl.

Aman did not arouse their curiosity and did not allow anyone to see the girl. Aman's wife came to protest in anger to keep the girl.
Aman threatened that if he went too far, he would not have time to abandon her like his previous wife.

Aman came to his cottage at night. He said that if he married Aman, he would stop worshiping the demon gods and do as his lord said.

There was no sign of fear or apprehension on the girl's face. Only he made it clear that he was not allowed to be a disciple of the Lord. Aman smiled demonically.

He said that two roads are open for him. Not a single road will release him. Either he will marry Aman or his blood will be sacrificed to the demons in the next abandonment.

This is the first time Aman saw fear in the girl's eyes. The girl said that if such a thing happens, there will be a terrible danger in this group.

The Holy Spirit will turn away from them. There is no fear in Aman's eyes.

Just wanted to get the girl. However, he does not want to force the girl to suffer for some unknown reason.

The girl wants to welcome him. The greed for extra power and energy, the thought of stopping the demon worship has disappeared from my head.

The girl stood silently for a long time. Then he came forward slowly towards Aman. A lot has changed in appearance.

The atmosphere of the house has become mysterious in the light of the light hurricane. The form seems to be coming out of the girl's body. Aman is losing control.

The girl approached him and said, 'Do you love me?'

Anyone in the group would lose consciousness if they saw Aman's shy face. He said in fear, 'Yes'.
'But give it a try!

There are 8 idols that you worship. One big and 6 small. What you don't know is that the big vampire is the father and the rest are his children.

You sacrifice this blood for them. If you can, hide and take an idol from there and float it in the river!

Aman got up in surprise and stepped back, 'Impossible!

body of the girl. Black bunches of black cells are moving all over the body. I have no idea about its power.

I fear that even the innermost thoughts of my mind seem to know that. That demonic force will kill me at any moment!

You also have no idea about the holy power of my Lord. Test the power of my Lord.

With this, the girl took off her sari. Aman stared at the girl's body in amazement. The lust that is frozen in the mind has disappeared in an instant.

There is not even a speck of youth in the

Numerous small holes in them. This girl is not a woman or a man!

The body has many small roots sticking out of the body through the abdomen, breasts, and neck.

Pulling a few thin roots from there, he made a garland like a rope by twisting the lump with his hands. Then he put it on, Aman.

The cells that used to squirm in the body got lost inside the body.

A lustful body appeared there. The girl wrapped her clothes around her body again. He said to Aman, 'Go and do what I say. See the power of my Lord.

A man's body is shaking with terrible excitement. He went out with a hurricane to the forest where there are seven vampire statues.

He looked around, again and again, to see if anyone was watching him! No, no one!

Aman's pregnant wife was furious.

Another girl is taking his place. So he had been looking at Aman's cottage since evening.

At night when Aman entered the hut his whole body was burning. He wanted to set fire to the cottage and burn Aman and the girl alive. He seemed to calm himself down a bit.

He was surprised to see Aman leaving the hut in the middle of the night and entering the forest with a hurricane like a thief.

He thought Aman would not go out without having fun with the girl all night. She also took a hurricane in her hand and secretly followed her Husband.

CHAPTER 10:

Aman, the head of the group of vampire worshipers,

was so attracted to the beautiful woman who suddenly appeared in his house that in a few moments he no longer had any knowledge of Hitahita.

He doesn't even know what a terrible thing he is going to do.

He walked a long way in the light of the hurricane and appeared at their place of worship. There are 6 idols there.

He looked around again and saw that there was no one. This was the first time his whole body trembled. He realizes how big a risk he is going to take to test the power of an unknown force.

The vampire gods that have benefited them so far, have given them power. He is going to give up one of them.

The blood of the body is turning to ice thinking that what kind of punishment and curse may come down on them for abandoning the child of such a powerful demon. The legs are reluctant to move forward.

Once he looked at the necklace that the girl was wearing.

His mind became hard. Slowly proceeded to the statues. Even the smallest statue is about half its size.

He knows how much it weighs! Still, he hugged it in fear and went to raise it. Surprisingly, it weighs like a baby fox to him. You don't have to get any speed to get high.

He threw the hurricane and hugged the idol with both hands. Lonely reservoir all around.
Suddenly a light began to radiate from his necklace.

So enough to walk the path. He ran to the river bank. Everyone in the group is still asleep.
As he approached the river, his heartbeat increased again.

Suffering from conflict, whether he will do the job! At that moment, his wife's voice came from behind, 'What are you doing? Stop!

She is having difficulty running as she is pregnant. Yet he quickly came to Aman. 'Leave it where it came from. What a terrible danger you are bringing!

You know nothing, stupid girl! We don't need the help of these demons now. I have found a superpower. That power will save us. ' Amin sighed.

'You have been deceived. You must be doing these things in the words of that girl! She must be a deceiver, taking the form of a woman and leading us astray. We will all be in danger!

With their shouts, a sudden storm began to blow. Clouds are calling in the sky. It's not the rainy season.

The people of the group slowly started coming out of the cottage. The conversation by the river went to my ears.

Everyone rushed towards the hurricane.

Realizing what the group leader was going to do, they screamed. Repeatedly begged not to throw the idol in the water.

There was a strange feeling in Aman's body then. Once he looked at his cottage. His invisible eyes say that the beautiful girl is waiting for him.

If he abandons the idol, he will be reunited with it. He will be the most powerful man in the region.

Gradually he came close to the river water. The people of the group are rushing to stop him. He turned around and looked at the river. No more worries! He threw the idol in the water.

Everyone was stunned for a moment. People have forgotten to breathe. Everyone shouted together, 'Alas! Alas!

The roar of the clouds and the wind have stopped.

The water of the river where the statue fell is moving abnormally. What a force trying to pull Aman.

Aman's heart sank. He tore the necklace and threw it in the water.

Then he ran up to the shore. Surprised to see that the water of that place on the bank of the river is spinning in a circle. Turning around, the water moved away and a huge hole was created.

Light is being scattered from the sky. Meanwhile, a terrible roar came from the jungle.

The vampires have woken up! The roar came again. A strange roar came out of the hole created in the river as a response! What's going on!

The terrible storm began. Nature is blowing in anger.
Everyone started running towards their cottages.

Aman also rushed to his hut with his wife and appeared.

He entered the cottage and saw that the girl was not there! But the same! Inside the house, there is a thick, dead tree!

Where did this tree come from in his cottage!

Aman and his wife stared at the tree in amazement at the flickering light of the hurricane.

Suddenly he noticed a part of the bark of the tree trembling.

Two eyes came out from there through a leak, a huge face came out just below him. Aman's wife lost consciousness by screaming in fear.

Aman sat down on the ground in fear. A familiar voice came out of the mouth of the tree, 'Aman! You're a bad person!

But never regret what you did today. You saved the whole region by abandoning that vampire.

The power of the vampires was gradually increasing in your sacrifice.

And if you continued to worship these vampires for a while by sacrificing the blood of new people, they would get back all the energy they had lost which the great power of the jungle had taken away from them.

When they get power, they will spread their power and strength in all regions.

Violence, anger, and bloodshed spread everywhere. I'm not cheating.

I am not a woman or a man, there is no specific shape.

Great power has made me take any form so that I can lead people astray by deception and lies.

For a long time, I have been in this forest, in the river, how many people have been misled and prevented from coming to this region.

I have tried to keep away from those idols. I just failed to stop the people in your group. You have increased the power of that demon a lot by worshiping for so long.
After trying a lot, 'Aman', I was able to chat with you. No! You do not question the power of the great power!

But you have to finish what you started. By abandoning one of the seven demons, you and the people of your group became angry with them. Because whatever you throw at them in the river is the child of demonic power.

Now that demonic power will destroy you in anger, the child in your wife's womb, all the group including the wife will be destroyed by the demonic power, will curse. And there will be great chaos.

Only then will my Lord, the great holy power of the forest, appear. He will then curse those vampires again.

I commanded you to do this, so I was cursed. I must be a tree from now until I die. You too!

After saying so much, his eyes and face disappeared again.

Aman is feeling that there is a terrible earthquake all around. Storms are blowing along with it, strong waves and the sound of water coming from the direction of the river.

A terrible blood-chilling roar is coming from inside the forest. And the screams and groans of the people of the group can be heard.

Aman was left to understand what terrible consequences were going to happen. His wife is still lying unconscious on the floor.

Suddenly he trembled. Her stomach is shaking terribly. Wisdom is returning to his wife! Okay!

The girl came out with a hole in her stomach. A few roots! Aman shouted back!

All the skin on his wife's body turned black as soon as he saw it.

In a few moments, the rice of the house was broken and the girl was transformed into a thick tree.

There is another small tree standing next to it. Aman felt his body getting confused.

Thousands of insects are running inside his stomach, throat, body, blood, and veins! She is groaning in terrible pain.

His body is swollen.
He lost knowledge, vision, and speech. He became a tall, thick, lifeless tree.

Many of the rest of the group are instantly turned into trees by the curse of the demon, and some of them are afflicted with a terrible disease.

Their flesh-eating insects continue to grow inside the body. Which comes out of the body eating all the organs.

They die. The rest were swept away by the terrible current rising from the river.

Some of them may have survived. The current of the river swept away the distant village.

This is how the demon worship group is destroyed. The vampire loses his ability to use his power directly, and anger people.

The jungle superpower then cursed the vampire and his son into a deep place in the jungle and transformed them into trees.

Then a hundred years passed.

The vampires are slowly regaining power. Gives birth to a vampire male.

That fooling Sakina traps everyone in the village and collects the bodies of hundreds of dead women in the hollow of a huge tree to free the demonic power!

CHAPTER 11 LAST PART:

Current time. There was a great commotion in the whole village of Sakina. In the last few months alone, 30 women have gone missing in their village.

No one in the village has any doubt in their minds that they have disappeared after going to that forest.

More than 20 youths have been killed by wild animals while searching for missing women in broad daylight.

No one could find the monstrous tree that the women were talking about. Only women find it at night. Which fulfills all their desires.

Although the bodies of the youths were found, there is no news of missing women. Tensions have also risen in nearby villages.

Many of their women have also gone missing in recent months. Everyone is looking for the missing girls like crazy.

They started preaching everywhere so that no one would go to the forest out of greed.

It was not difficult for anyone to understand that a strange force dragged the girls to the forest at night.

So everyone started guarding the women of the house.

The group started to stay on the edge of the forest in the evening.

Whenever he sees a woman coming towards the forest, he seizes her by force and sends her home.

Sakina never went to the forest again after the day she came back with the roots. For the first few days, his mind was on the unknown young man. He hoped that maybe the young man would come and see him.

But as the days went by, the women of the village secretly became anxious to fulfill their desires by praying to the tree.
It seemed to be successful effortlessly. But in the meantime, the number of missing women began to increase.

Sakina felt a sense of remorse. That is why the women of the village came to know about the tree.

The young man used it as bait to accomplish a nefarious purpose! Maybe his father got better, but in return, the whole village was in danger.

Moreover, at best, the young man appeared as soon as the animal left the forest.

After the young man left, the huge white beast arrived.

He heard from the villagers a description of a terrifying animal that would enter the village at night to kill their pets.

It is similar to the beast he saw! However, the young man is polymorphic! Sometimes it becomes an animal, sometimes it becomes a man! What is possible!

Even the villagers nowadays think that Sakina is responsible for all their suffering. They often come to Hossain Mia's house to scold him. Especially the village elders.

He was called a witch and a ghost worshiper. Sakina cries. He does not understand, how to answer!

Night In the middle of the forest. A middle-aged woman is being bitten by a huge white beast.

With the radiance of the beast's fierce gaze, he advanced into the hollow next to the thick roots of the huge tree. No one can guess from the outside how big and how deep the inside is.

He threw the woman's body at the pile of 96 more bodies. As soon as he came out of the hole, he let out a huge roar. This roar of joy, of pride.

Then all the soil in the forest shook. Some light began to scatter in this part of the forest.

In that light, it is clear that the huge lifeless leafless tree is trembling. His huge skin fell from his body.

Numerous cells came out from there while chirping. Numerous small, long, black insects are emerging from them.

Out of there came two small eyes and a large face. Both eyes are shining. It made a huge noise, and the whole forest shook.

Then he looked at a small white creature leaning in front of him. The heavy voice growled.

'You played a great game, son! You will be my most powerful child when I regain all my strength.

It roared again. Suddenly some of the thick, leafy, lifeless monstrous trees in the vicinity trembled. They also want to say something.

You have deposited 99 women's bodies there, and one is needed.

This time the whole body of the animal began to tremble. Hair on the body, and sharp nails disappeared.

It turned out to be a handsome young man. Hatumure sat down again.

In a trembling voice, he addressed the monstrous tree and said, 'Lord, great mighty! I tried everything.

I apologize for the delay. But the villagers are now quite cautious. No one is allowed in here. I can't even bind them directly to your order. I have even given up my hunger.

I did not attack the locality! But people are very greedy! They take one way or another to enter the forest. So there will be no shortage of women for your sacrifice.
It will take time though! But it will be complete only if there is another woman.

Yes! But I blocked the jungle path. No other woman will be able to reach me even if she enters the forest.

You don't even have to hunt it down in the guise of an animal! '
'I mean, Lord! The rest is a woman!

'There are 99 bodies here! But none of them are teenagers! The last woman we need is a teenager. You will bring him from the locality.

The young man's face went completely dry. He understood who he was talking about. He leaned down quietly.

Seeing that, the bark again covered the huge tree. It turned into a dead tree. The young man stood still for a few moments, his mind swayed by the conflict.

Then he shouted in anger. The moment turned into a white beast. I started running in the locality. He has to go to Sakina's house. He will not disobey the order at this last moment.

Midnight in the village. Sakina woke up startled by the sound of someone knocking on the door. Who came this night, she thought.

As soon as I opened the door, I was startled and stepped back a few feet. I

s he dreaming? Standing there is the young man in whose love he went mad one day.

Seeing him again, he had to admit that there is no other such handsome man in the world. What Maya in this face, who could be more holy!

The young man motioned for her to go with him. Sakina came out of the house in satisfaction. Going a little farther, the young man hid. Teenager Sakina is by his side.

The young man stepped forward and gently touched Sakina's chin. Said, 'Forgive me, I have not been able to come so far. But now you have to go to the forest with me. We both started a terrible game, we have to end it.

That huge tree is responsible for all the women who have gone missing in this area. A white beast helped him. Their purpose will be fulfilled only if they can arrest another woman.

In the forest, the demonic power will get back their full power. Then only destruction and destruction.

'I don't understand anything you say!'
Sakina looked confused.

'Nothing to understand, you just believe
me. Come with me Only you, as the parent
can know for sure.
Sakina fell into conflict.

Why should he believe the man again!

But it is also true that he can feel that a big
danger is coming to the village.

Moreover, there is something in this young
man that cannot be done. He agreed to go.

The young man silently took her to the end
of the village. Then the jungle began to
walk in the opposite direction.

Sakina was surprised and asked, 'Where
are you taking me here, not the jungle!'

'We should not go to the forest this way.
We will go to the bank of the canal.

From there I will fall into a river by boat, that river will take me to a big river, that river will turn around and reach the forest. Don't ask any more questions. I wish you all the best.

The young man started walking again, and Sakina was following him.
At the end of the forest, at the beginning of the village, a big white animal appeared.

He transformed his body into the body of a young man. Some people were guarding the road against behind.

He entered the village unnoticed by them. Sakina felt a little love for the girl. But it is not so dark that all the hard work of so many days will be in vain.

He has to forget the girl and take her to the forest.
Quiet night. He appeared in front of Sakina's house.

He was surprised to see the door open. Slowly entering the house on foot, Sakina is nowhere!

In one room only his father is sleeping. Where did he go so late at night?

He could not be found anywhere around the house. He has the power of an animal.

He dried a cloth used by Sakina. Then he leaned down and looked at the ground. That's all he got.

The impressions are gone. A little farther on, he was surprised to see the footprints of two people.

One Sakina, the other who! The footprints on the top seem very familiar.

Following in his footsteps, he started running fast. If he goes back to the body of the animal, there will be a danger, so he is running as a human being.

The young man came running to the bank of a canal. A boat can be seen in the distance, two men and women are getting on the boat. Going a little further from behind, he was completely stunned by what he saw.

A young boat with Sakina. That young man is no one else. She! Yeah Al that sounds pretty crap to me, Looks like BT ain't for me either. How is this possible?

Who else in this jungle rivals the vampire man in the guise of his son who will come and snatch his prey by trickery!

Or seeing that his father did not trust him, the vampire man has created another man exactly like him! Nothing is understood. He looked at the boat.

The young man in the boat hugged Sakina tightly before Sakina realized anything. He pressed hard on his chest. Sakina lost consciousness.

The young man put him in the boat and picked him up.
From a distance, the young man ran to the bank of the canal.

The young man sitting in the boat also looked at the shore in amazement. He shouted, 'Who are you?

Why did you take my form? Where are you going with Sakina? Who is your lord?

The same-looking young man sitting in the boat laughed and said, 'You are late, friend, tell your vampire father that you will be destroyed again, the child of the great holy power of the forest has returned.

Goodbye, get ready for destruction. '
Saying this, he released the boat. Standing on the bank, the young man began to squirm. He does not understand why he is so afraid to go into the water.

He screamed in anger. Turned into that ferocious monstrous white beast.

A young man like her, sitting in a boat, turned into a woman. The beast was amazed to see the beautiful woman.

Is this the deception that has cursed him for so many years? He did not become a cursed tree!

How was it released! Surely deceit has been cursed for a hundred years in the same way that his lord was slowly being freed from the curse.
The boat is moving at its speed. The beast is running after it along the bank of the canal.

The boat crossed the canal and fell into a small river. The boat did not hide from the eyes of the beast for a moment.

This time the boat came to the big river. The river flows into the forest.

The beast was surprised that the girl in the boat never tried to go behind the beast with Sakina.

The boat is moving only at a distance from the shore so that the animal cannot jump and climb on it. Sakina's senses have not yet returned.

The girl with the oar hand is looking at the animal from time to time with a sly smile which makes the animal angrier.

Suddenly the beast noticed another buck from the river in front. As a result, he could no longer follow the boat.

To get to the level of the boat, he has to turn around and take another path.

Impossible to get into the water! However, the boat will be hidden from view for a while.

He ran along the bank of the river on the right side with all his might, ran straight along the bank of the end of the bank, and then turned left and ran along the bank and reached the bank of the river.

Disappointed, he looked around. Where did the boat go!

He started running towards the front in a non-stop manner. If it is hidden, it is impossible to find it.

What will it do with Sakina! Why did her vampire lord pressure her to abandon Sakina as the last woman! She's upset.

But after going some distance, he regained his life as if he could see the boat. He rushed there and appeared. Sakina is in the boat.

That girl is gone. Where did he leave Sakina! Gradually he came back in human form.

If you want to reach the boat, you have to swim in the water. But he will not go down into the water. He started calling Sakina.
The girl regained consciousness after calling a few times.

He looked at the young man with a drowsy look. Said, 'Did I fall asleep? Why my whole body is in pain!

I can't move! Where did you bring me! Get down to the shore! '

The young man became desperate! Realizing that Sakina doesn't remember anything after getting on the boat.

What a smell of danger coming to the nose.
He said to Sakina, 'You push the boat a little! The boat will come ashore! '

Sakina got up and snorted, reaching for the seat with great difficulty. Pushing it, the boat came ashore.

The young man jumped up and sat on the boat. He went to pick up Sakina. Sakina's face hardened in an instant.

Inhuman anger in the eyes.

He grabbed the young man's hand tightly and put him in the boat with him.

The young man flinched. Before she knew it, Sakina pushed the oar of the boat hard. With a single push, the boat sank into the river, a long way from the shore.

Seeing the water around, the young man's chest trembled. He realized that he did not have a single drop of energy in his body.

Sakina is still holding his hand tightly. So much power in the hands of the girl! Sakina looked him in the eye and said, 'I am not Sakina! That's Sakina! '

The young man pointed his finger at a tree and saw Sakina lying unconscious in a bush on the bank of the river. Then who is this?

At that moment, Sakina's teenage body was transformed into the body of an adult girl. The look also changed.

This is the girl who took Sakina in her boat and brought her here.

The girl said, 'I'm not cheating. Disciple of the great holy power. Sakina girl is just a trick. My purpose was to bring you here.

You are the son of that ferocious vampire. You are responsible for the deaths of countless people, including 99 innocent women.

The demon cleverly made you into a mixture of animals and humans.

Because these two classes cannot be directly cursed by the Holy Spirit.

You have created great chaos in this world. That's why nothing was done to you.

Although you did everything at the behest of the demon! But it cannot be cursed because it did nothing directly.

Only if you put this teenage girl in the hole will the vampire get back all the power. This is how I let it be! Great power has freed me from this curse. No, Sakina is not a special woman! Instead, he would get strength even if he stuck someone in a hole.

But she chose Sakina as the last woman to test your loyalty. And this is my advantage to trap you.

You are his son. If you die now, all plans will fail. 99 murders will be blamed on that vampire tree and its offspring.

All the demonic forces will be destroyed by the curse of the great holy power. Maybe not for eternity, but for a long time. Yes, I will be cursed again for killing you!

The young man shouted. He looked like an animal. But Budd was late.
The girl jumped down and grabbed the edge of the boat. The boat capsized in an instant.

The young man felt as if his whole body was on fire. Both of them including the boat sank in the water.

The water there began to turn in a circle. The great hole was created.

At the same time, a great roar came from the jungle. The whole jungle cried out.

Screams also came out of the hole created in the river. The quake shook the area. Sakina regained consciousness.

He was startled by such a strange roar, the speed of the storm, the roar of the waves. Fear began to run like a blind man.

The sky began to burst with lightning. He smashed a huge leaf and a lifeless tree into pieces.

Six such trees in his vicinity were shattered by lightning and caught fire.

The bodies of 99 women in the cave were burnt to ashes in the huge fireplace of the big tree.

The jungle continued to burn until the rain came.
Sakina was the only one who could come running into the village.

But how much of what happened in the jungle remained in his head, and how much or what future generations will know!